For Erica Wakerly

Copyright © 2009 by Polly Dunbar

First U.S. edition 2009

Library of Congress Cataloging-in-Publication Data
Dunbar, Polly.
Doodle Bites / Polly Dunbar.
— 1st U.S. ed.
p. cm.
Summary: Doodle the alligator awakens feeling "bitey,"
and soon all of the animal friends are in tears.
ISBN 978-0-7636-4327-0
[1. Behavior — Fiction. 2. Animals — Fiction.] I. Title.
PZ7.D89445Doo 2009
[E] — dc22   2009000895

2 4 6 8 10 9 7 5 3 1

Printed in China

This book was typeset in Gill Sans MT Schoolbook.
The illustrations were done in mixed media.

Candlewick Press
99 Dover Street
Somerville, Massachusetts 02144

visit us at www.candlewick.com

Tilly and
her friends
all live
together in
a little yellow
house. . . .

Doodle
Bites

Polly Dunbar

CANDLEWICK PRESS

Doodle

woke up

feeling

BITEY!

After she had CHOMPED her breakfast,

she CHEWeD the mail.

She even CRUNCHED and

MUNCHED on the sofa.

While she was **NIBBLING** the lamp,

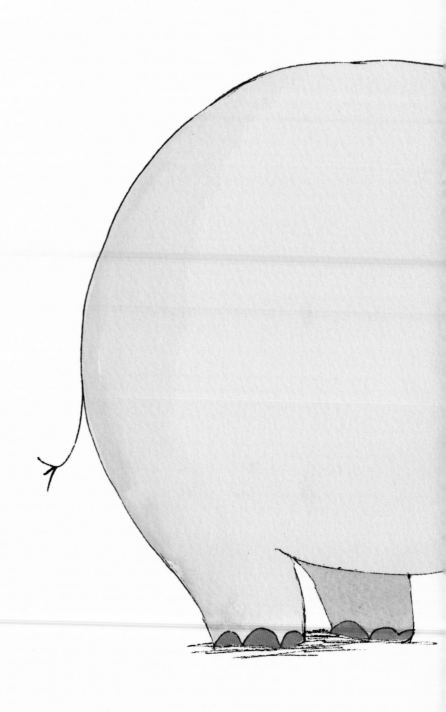

Doodle spied something very good to bite.

"OW!"

shouted Tumpty.

"That's my bottom!"

Tumpty was very upset.

"You shouldn't bite
your friends,"
said Tilly.
"It's not
nice."

"Mmm,"
said Doodle.

BITEY! BITEY!

Then Tumpty stomped on Doodle's tail.

"**YOW!**"
shouted Doodle.
"That's my
tail!"

"You shouldn't
stomp on
your friends,"
said Tilly,
"even if they
bite you.

It's not nice."

Tumpty was crying.

Doodle was

crying.

Even Hector started crying.

"Don't worry—I'm here!" said Pru,
and she gave Tumpty an
extra-large bandage
for his bottom.

Tilly gave Doodle
a bandage for
her tail.

Hector
and Tiptoe
got bandages too.

Then
Pru kissed
everyone
all better.

Even Doodle!

"I'm sorry
I stomped
on your tail,"
said Tumpty.

"I'm sorry
I bit your
bottom,"
said Doodle.

Hooray!

Everyone was happy again!

But
Doodle still felt
just a little bit bitey!

"Oh, no, you don't!"

said Tumpty.

Pru gave Doodle an
extra-special
bandage.

No more bitey bitey!